An Elephant
Called Butterfly

* * *

marian hailey-moss and lois meredith

ISBN: 1502817306
ISBN 13: 9781502817303

Illustrations by Marc Chalvin

we lovingly dedicate this book
to
all the elephants

may they continue to enrich and inspire us

1

* * *

In Africa, a baby elephant was born.

The heavy rains prepared the way, and a rainbow appeared in the sky. The ostriches and hornbills, the hibiscus and forest jasmine, and even the insects rejoiced. The sun's golden orb smiled in the sky. And the elephants danced in slow motion to a song from the beginning of time.

There was soothing mother's milk to be had. The baby elephant's mother knew when her little one was hungry and when she felt good or bad. Her mother was a lifeline to a rhapsody of movement, sound, smell, sight, and taste.

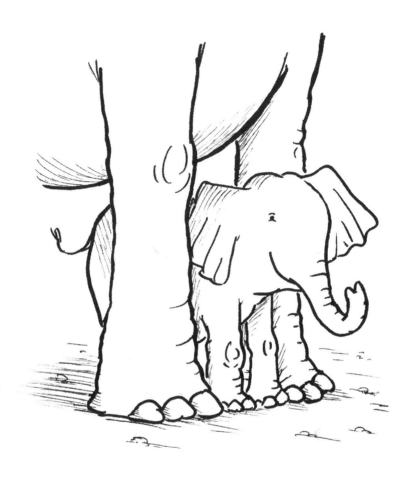

There was an amazing trunk to explore. The baby could use it to pick up dirt and sticks and to hang on to her mother's tail. Her mother could scoop water with her trunk and drink. When the baby tried the same, hers made squiggles and squirts instead. The grown-ups blew water from their trunks to get the baby clean after the mud baths that kept her skin healthy.

They roamed in a herd—her mother and about ten other females who were all related. There were sisters, aunts, cousins, and grandmothers. There were a few young males who would later leave to form a group of bachelors. The oldest female, the matriarch, was the leader and the boss. That's how it is in the elephant world. The new baby stayed close to her mother and the grown-up females. It was like being in a forest of big gray trees that shielded the baby from harm.

It had been three months, and oh, there was so much more to learn. She would grow up beautiful and strong like the others.

One day her mother lingered a little behind the herd. She was enjoying a place that had a stream surrounded by high brush and acacia trees. The baby thought the trees looked strange, not like the elephant forest that kept her safe.

They were there by themselves when something startled her mother. She urged her baby to run back with her to the herd, but the baby couldn't run fast enough so the mother stopped running.

There was a flash of silver. Her mother's cry tore all color from the sky, from the birds and trees, from the flowers and insects. The ground around them became soaked in red. She was alone—a three-month-old baby elephant. And then everything went black.

2

* * *

Thabo heard the helicopter overhead. It was bringing another baby elephant. Another orphan. Another life to save. Poachers brought grief to elephant families. Elephant tusks brought dirty money to greedy outlaws who were willing to break the law and kill innocent elephants for profit. If the mother is killed, a baby that is not yet two years old is doomed to die in the wild.

Thabo was twelve and had lived at the sanctuary ever since he could walk. He loved the baby elephants. He felt a kinship with them, for he knew what it was like to be an orphan. Malaria had taken his birth parents when he was a year old. A family friend brought him to the sanctuary where the owner and his wife had taken him in.

Thabo helped in the nursery. He was only a boy and had his studies to attend to, but he liked to help the keepers with their job. The keepers were with the babies twenty-four hours a day—on rotation, of course. They fed the babies every ten minutes, because that's how often baby elephants nurse in the wild. Babies, for the first year, have only mother's milk for their diet. In the sanctuary, they were fed a special recipe of baby formula and coconut oil.

The helicopter was landing now. The door opened, and the baby elephant was carried on a stretcher to the nursery. Some babies don't survive the journey—they are too scared and too sick. But this one survived the transport. The next twenty-four hours would be crucial. The baby's spirit was the most important thing. If the baby gave up wanting to live, no loving, no milk, no medicine on earth could boost its shattered will.

Thabo followed it into the stall that was prepared for the arrival. The stall was spotlessly clean with fresh hay on the ground. The first thing was to get the baby settled. She wouldn't sit down but kept walking in circles. She was dazed and confused. The keeper was trying to help her focus on him—the pretend mother—by touching and coaxing her, but it was all to no avail.

Thabo reached out to the baby. A glimmer of light came into the young elephant's eyes upon seeing Thabo. Her gaze moved him deeply. "Please, let Bitri try," he begged.

Bitri was the elephants' favorite keeper. He could soothe the most anguished of animals. He was tall and skinny—to them, just one skinny elephant.

Bitri arrived at the stall, and by midnight the baby was able to lie down. Bitri and Thabo stayed beside her throughout the night. The next morning, Bitri held the bottle of formula from behind a gray blanket. The sanctuary keepers use the blanket to copy the look and feel of the baby's mother. Otherwise, there would be no accepting the bottle. The baby began to drink! She had made it over the first hurdle.

The baby's ears were bigger than most and rippled while she nursed. They were like delicate, fluttering wings.

"Let's call her Butterfly," Thabo said.

Bitri smiled and nodded *yes*.

3

* * *

It was Saturday and Emma sat in the courtyard garden. She loved being there. It was a little oasis of nature where she could daydream. There were oak trees, winding pathways, and lovely flowering red azaleas along with tall green bushes. It was quite out of the ordinary for a New York City apartment house. What would she do for the day? She and Rufus had been for their morning walk. Rufus was a blond terrier mix—a rescue that she had adopted from the local shelter. Rufus was her best friend, Emma's shadow. She told him everything, and he always seemed to understand. Right now he was upstairs snoozing in the family apartment.

Emma was trying to decide if she should practice the piano or phone her friend across the street. If her friend was home, they could go together to get some cinnamon rolls. She decided on some time with her friend. As she was getting ready to leave, she saw a boy about her age standing at the garden door. She waved hello. "Are you looking for someone?"

"No, just at the garden," he said. "My name is Thabo." He was trying to find any similarity between the greens of a New York courtyard garden and the African plains. It was a challenging task.

"Did you say *Thabo*?" asked Emma, making sure she'd heard him correctly.

"Yes, it means *joy* in Sesato, which is the language of the Basuto people. That's in South Africa."

"Oh...hi! I'm Emma."

"What does your name mean?"

"I guess it just means...me."

"I bet it means *pretty*," he said, smiling. Thabo had started to find his confidence with girls when he turned twelve a few months ago. He walked over to where she was standing.

Emma caught her breath. She had never been told so boldly by a boy that she was pretty. And she was wearing her glasses, too. She cast her eyes down for a moment and then asked if he were living here now. He explained that he and his adoptive father had come to New York City from Kenya. They were staying here at Astor Court with friends. His father was to give a speech at the United Nations. The speech was about protecting elephants.

Emma didn't know that elephants needed protecting. They seemed so big and strong. Thabo agreed that one wouldn't think so. However, he explained in another twenty years, there might be no more elephants at all.

"That would be terrible," said Emma. "But at least we'd still have cats and dogs."

"It is much better to have all the animals, don't you think?" said Thabo.

"Yes, of course," said Emma. She stole a look at Thabo as he turned his gaze back to the garden. He was very thin, but also strong, it seemed, and he was handsome. She didn't know much about elephants. But for now they seemed a good way to know Thabo better. "Why do elephants need protecting?"

"They are big and strong, but they are gentle creatures. One of their biggest threats is the poachers killing them for their tusks."

"How horrible," said Emma. "What are the tusks used for?"

Thabo explained that tusks are pure ivory. "Poachers can get a lot of money for them. They are sold on the black market."

"What's that?" Emma asked.

"It means they're sold secretly, against the law."

Emma's eyes widened.

"China is the largest buyer, but there are big illegal markets in the United States, too, and all over the world. Ivory gets carved into art objects and jewelry, and people pay lots of money for it," Thabo explained. "Like the pendant you're wearing now." He pointed at her necklace.

Emma felt her cheeks flushing red. The butterfly pendant was a gift for her eleventh birthday from her parents. She'd never thought it had anything to do with elephants.

"This was a special present," Emma said.

"I'm sorry," said Thabo. "It's made of ivory."

Emma was taken aback. She'd had no idea. Thabo told her his adoptive parents had a wildlife preserve. And on the preserve they had a sanctuary where they helped injured and orphaned elephants. "Many people don't know that ivory comes at the price of an elephant's life," he told her. "There is one killed every fifteen minutes."

Thabo sighed and took out his cell phone.

"Here's a photo of our latest orphan. We are trying to save her and help her to someday go back to the wild. It's still not certain she will live."

"Oh, she's beautiful," said Emma. "And she looks so helpless and innocent."

"She *is* helpless. She's just a baby—even though she weighs three hundred and twenty-five pounds! That's big for a human, but it's average for a three-month-old elephant calf." Thabo glanced once again at Emma's pendant. "We named her Butterfly."

Emma was silent for a minute. Who was this strange young person? It felt like her day had turned upside down. He had such a passion for elephants. She liked being with him. She bit her lip and gently unfastened the pendant from around her neck and put it in her pocket. "Would you like me to show you the neighborhood?"

"Yes, I'd like that," said Thabo. "Can we meet tomorrow? I have to go with my father now."

"Tomorrow, then."

4

* * *

That night as Emma was getting ready for bed, she took the butterfly pendant from her pocket. There in the palm of her hand, it looked different. After meeting Thabo, the beauty of the pendant had faded. She knew her parents wouldn't have given her anything made from ivory if they had known where it came from. Elephants and their troubles seemed so far away from New York City. She gently put the pendant in its red velvet box. It was a treasure that she would never wear again.

Emma turned around to where Rufus was lying by her bed, fast asleep. She loved him even though he tended to snore a lot. Animals were easy to love even though they weren't perfect.

She climbed into bed. She was happy to have a new friend in Thabo. And such an interesting friend. All the way from Africa. That photo of Butterfly—she was such a sweet creature! Emma pulled the blanket up to her chin.

It had been a special day. Just thinking about it brought a smile to her face.

"Emma," said her mother as she peeked into her daughter's bedroom. "You forgot to say good night."

"Oh, Mom!"

Her mother bent down to kiss Emma's cheek. "Good night, precious. Keep my love tucked under your pillow."

"G'night, Mom," she said a little absentmindedly as she began to fall into a deep sleep. Strange images floated in and out of her dream world. Animals of all kinds, small and large, wild and tame—alligators and cows, lions and antelopes, dogs and elephants. They moved across the sky and the land, a colorful, changing tapestry.

How amazing they all are, thought Emma. The animals were making the sounds they usually made, but suddenly she could understand what they were saying!

"Thabo! Thabo!" a voice was calling out from the garden. It sounded like both a horn and a bleating.

Emma ran to the window and saw a baby elephant pacing back and forth.

"What are you doing?" she asked as she flung open her bedroom window.

"I'm looking for Thabo. Have you seen him?"

"Butterfly?" Emma asked in amazement.

"No, Thabo! I'm looking for Tha—"

"I mean, are *you* Butterfly?"

The baby elephant said that she was indeed Butterfly, even though it was an odd name for an elephant. How did Emma know it was she? Emma told her that Thabo had shown her a picture.

At the mention of Thabo's name, the baby elephant wailed all the louder.

"Shhhhh," said Emma. "You'll wake everybody."

"How can I, when it's daylight?"

"Oh, so it is," said Emma. "I'll be right down. Come on, Rufus!"

Emma threw on some clothes, and went quickly to the garden. Baby Butterfly was pacing back and forth. Her trunk was making loop-de-loops in the air, and her skinny tail was swinging.

"How did you get past Jack the doorman?" asked Emma.

"He was busy helping a lady put her groceries in the elevator when I walked through the lobby," Butterfly explained.

Just then, Thabo came to the garden door.

"Butterfly!"

Baby Butterfly was beyond happy. And if ever there was a joyous meeting between a baby elephant and a boy, this was it. Butterfly wrapped her trunk around Thabo's chest and around his arm, and then around his neck and back to his chest again.

"I missed you," said Thabo as he hugged the baby elephant.

With all the excitement going on, Rufus started barking. Emma introduced Butterfly to Rufus, and then Butterfly tapped Rufus on the back with her trunk to say hello.

Thabo wanted to know how Butterfly knew he was here in New York City. She reminded him that elephants have a keen intuition and are very loyal. So New York City was as obvious a spot as the trunk on her face.

And then Butterfly became serious.

"I was hoping we might find a safe place for me to live when I grow up."

Thabo was surprised. He asked why Butterfly didn't want to live in Africa. It was her home. "I would always be afraid that the poachers would come back. I remember the day that my mother..."

Thabo nodded sadly. Now he understood all too well. He looked at Emma. "Elephants never forget, you know."

But what to do? Butterfly certainly couldn't stay at Astor Court—first of all because of her size, and second, the garden would only be a snack for an elephant's appetite. Thabo told Emma that a grown elephant eats about 320 pounds of plant material, fruits, and grain in a day, and drinks thirty gallons of water. It was out of the question.

"What about the circus?" asked Emma.

Thabo told Emma that he had heard things about the circus that didn't sound so wonderful, but he had never been to one. "We could go see for ourselves," Thabo suggested.

They found themselves in the subway—a real New York City experience! Butterfly was not comfortable. She felt closed in, and she didn't like being underground with no sunlight. This was not like her home in Africa! She was startled by the mariachi band that abruptly entered and began playing an old Mexican folk song as they peddled for cash. Butterfly's tail began to swish nervously. Curiously, most people didn't even seem to notice. In New York, so many strange things happened that an elephant taking the subway didn't attract attention. They did overhear a nearby woman whisper to her companion, "Must be one of those new elephant service dogs." Butterfly extended her trunk, opened her nostrils, and breathed a sigh of relief as the door opened onto the circus arena.

***

"Wow!" said Emma. "We have front-row seats."

"I'm really at the circus!" said Butterfly in awe of it all.

Thabo thought Butterfly should stand in the aisle. It would be a tight squeeze to fit into a seat. Rufus could sit on Emma's lap.

"Oh, my!" said Butterfly. "This place is big!"

Emma noticed again that no one seemed surprised that there was a baby elephant in the audience. Maybe they thought she was part of the show.

"We got here just in time," said Thabo. "The lights are dimming."

The arena went dark, and a deep voice announced, "The best show on Earth!"

There was a blast of trumpets and then rousing music. In a blaze of light, the procession began. The clowns led the way, with funny wigs, funny clothes, and funny painted faces. They were jumping, running, pushing carts, and pushing one another. The ponies, with feathers on their heads, pranced around the arena. The lion tamer was waving and pulling a cage with lions. There were contortionists in pretzel poses being pulled on carts, and acrobats and jugglers, and finally...the elephants.

"Oh! Oh! Oh!" Butterfly gasped. And her trunk made loop-de-loops.

The elephants were a wonderful sight. They towered over everyone and everything. They were bedecked with jeweled crowns on their foreheads and jeweled, colorful throws over their bodies. Trapeze artists in glittering costumes rode on the elephants' backs. Butterfly waved her trunk as they passed by. Thabo put his hand on Butterfly's side to calm her down.

Then the show began. The clowns were first. There was a bang followed by a column of smoke. About twenty clowns climbed through the smoke out of a small car.

The lights dimmed. In the darkness the announcer's voice said, "And now for the highlight of our show (drum roll)...the elephants—Bumba, Mumba, and Rrrrumba!"

Butterfly squealed elephant sounds of delight. The audience went quiet. There was a pause and then the spotlights shone on three elephants. Their costumes glittered and glistened. They moved slowly and gracefully like giant ballerinas. A trainer dressed in red leggings, high black boots, and a white blouse carried a black baton, waved to the audience, and then gestured to the elephants. Three women in dazzling red, white, and blue sequined costumes made their entrance. They waved to the audience, and the elephants greeted them by standing on their back legs. Then the elephants each put one foot on a block and turned in unison. They played catch with colorful beach balls. Last but not least, the most difficult trick of all—handstands. "Oh! Oh!" cried Butterfly. Thabo and Emma sat forward on their seats. The audience gasped. One elephant couldn't keep her balance and fell. The elephant struggled, tried again, and finally made it. The audience cheered.

The elephants then lifted the young women with their trunks and danced around the arena to waltz music. They waltzed out of the arena through a tunnel while the young women waved good-bye. The trainer took a solo bow and with a flourish ran out the exit. Over the loudspeaker, the voice of the announcer boomed once again: *"Bumba, Mumba, and Rrrrumba!"*

The audience roared.

Well, Butterfly now knew this was *it*—the circus! This was the safe place to grow up, and she would make children happy and have fun. Thabo and Emma were excited, too. It seemed the circus was a good choice after all—with the bonus of lights, sparkle, and excitement.

"Oh, I could dance. I'm so happy!" said Butterfly. "Let's go backstage and try to find the elephants."

"Why not?" said Thabo and Emma.

"Let's go down the ramp," said Emma. "There's some light there." Suddenly, they were in a hall going around the building. They walked a very long way and came to an open door. They tiptoed in and saw in the dim light... the elephants!

***

"Oh, we found you!" exclaimed Butterfly, almost out of breath. "My name is Butterfly, and this is Thabo, Emma, and Rufus. We think you're wonderful. And I want to join the circus."

"Another starry-eyed fan," grumbled Bumba, looking up from her trough.

"Little do they know." Rumba rolled her eyes and snorted in agreement. The two elephants went back to eating their dinner of hay, straw, apples, celery, and carrots. The large elephant in front looked Butterfly up and down and finally spoke softly.

"Where's your mother, kid?"

"Poachers killed her."

"And who are these people?"

"They're my friends."

"I see...friends, huh?"

Thabo and Emma began to notice how dark it was in the room. Rufus stood closer to Emma. But Butterfly's face was shining with hope.

"Butterfly, or whatever your name is, you'd better 'fly' away," said the large elephant. "This is no place for you. Take a look at our ankles here."

"Yes, they're very pretty," said Butterfly, trying her best to be polite.

"Ha! Did you hear that, girls? Pretty! These are chains, kid! They're not bracelets." The other two elephants went on with their meal and didn't look up.

Butterfly was embarrassed but continued, "I thought maybe you'd talk to the higher-ups and tell them that I was ready."

"Oh, kid, you don't know anything, do you?" Mumba turned to the other two elephants and asked, "Should I tell her what life in the circus is really like?" They nodded and kept eating. Mumba adjusted her body and cleared her throat. "We were orphans like you—Rumba and Bumba here and myself. But we didn't have friends. We had trainers."

Thabo thought the way Mumba said "trainers" didn't sound promising.

"We were stolen in Thailand from our mothers when we were only a year old. Our mothers were helpless to do anything. Natives, hired through the exotic animal industry, shipped us to a circus camp here in the USA. We were scared and alone. That was just the beginning. Here, trainers would take the place of our mothers. Instead of love and rewards, they used fear and pain."

Butterfly was beginning to feel queasy. This meeting with the elephants wasn't going so well. In a small voice she asked, "What did they do?"

"First of all," said Mumba, "let me ask you this—when you were in the wild, did you ever see elephants doing handstands?" Before Butterfly could answer, she continued. "Did you see them playing ball, or wearing ballerina skirts, or turning in circles with one foot on a block?"

"Uh, well, I...I..." Butterfly found herself stuttering.

"I'll answer for you, kid," Mumba pressed on. "You didn't. It's unnatural for elephants to do such things. We elephants, like all animals, have an inborn dignity.

"Elephants—and don't ever forget this, Baby Butterfly—are in tune with nature. We are loving to our little ones and protect one another. We are highly intelligent, loyal, and peaceful. We are strong and can endure. But we are also fragile...fragile like a butterfly's wings. Our spirits can be crushed for profit. That's what you're looking at now. We are three elephants whose spirits have been crippled by being shackled for days, and beaten over and over and over again. All for handstands and ballerina skirts. Then there are hours of travel without food or water in stifling filthy trucks. That's the circus in a nutshell, Butterfly. That's the circus you say you want to join."

"Oh, please stop!" cried Butterfly. Tears were streaming down her face. Thabo and Emma were stunned. Rufus hid his tail between his legs.

"Can't you escape?" asked Butterfly, a bit pitifully.

"I'm truly sorry, kid. I wish—" Mumba stopped to listen. She heard footsteps approaching. She turned and saw a glimpse of their trainer coming toward them. His face was livid with rage. There was no telling what he would do. She turned toward Butterfly.

"The trainer is coming," Mumba whispered. "He's going to punish Bumba for falling. Don't let him see you.

Run, Butterfly and friends. Run and never, never, never turn back!"

They found the front door and escaped onto the street. It took a while before they caught their breath and calmed down.

"That was heartbreaking," said Thabo. "Are you all right, Butterfly?"

"I guess so."

But Emma realized that Butterfly was still crying. Large tears rolled down her cheeks. Emma felt terrible. She started crying, too.

***

"Emma! Emma!" It was Emma's mother, who had heard her daughter crying. She turned on the bedside lamp. Emma awoke with a start.

"Oh, Mama! Butterfly can't live at the circus."

Rufus was all in a dither. He thought they were going for a walk.

"Emma, what are you talking about?"

"Baby Butterfly...I dreamt that elephants are in chains and sometimes get beaten in the circus. Is that true?"

Her mother hesitated a moment. "Your dad and I were just talking about it the other day. We didn't think you could hear us, but maybe you did. That's why we haven't taken you to the circus in a while."

Emma was silent.

Her mother reached out to comfort her. "Do you want a glass of water or some hot cocoa?"

"No, I guess I'm okay."

"Try to get some sleep, Emma," said her mother. "And you know, your recital is coming up. We've got some practicing to do!"

"Okay, I'll try but..."

"Sweet dreams, now. See you in the morning."

"G'night, Mom."

Rufus settled back on his rug beside the bed and soon began snoring.

But Emma couldn't fall asleep right away. She kept thinking about those elephants at the circus and about Butterfly.

5

* * *

The next morning, Emma sat down at the piano to practice, but her mind was not on her music. She kept making mistakes. Her mother called to her from the next room.

"Emma, pay attention to your left hand! Bach is all in the left hand." Emma's mother knew music very well. She taught piano at the nearby music school.

"Bach is too hard to play. There's just too much going on," Emma called back, exasperated.

"Let me show you something," said her mother. But when she came into the living room, Emma had stopped playing and was staring at the piano keys.

"Are these made of ivory?" asked Emma.

"Of course," replied her mother. "This is my old baby grand piano. The very best."

"Are the keys made from elephant tusks?"

"Why, yes. That's what ivory is—elephant tusks."

"Did they kill an elephant to make this piano?"

"My understanding, Emma, is when this piano was made, they used only the tusks of elephants who had died of disease or old age," said her mother. "Nowadays, many pianos have plastic keys."

"Mom, do we have other things made of ivory?" Emma wanted to know.

"I...I don't know." Emma's mother seemed genuinely confused. "Probably Grandmother's candlesticks. They are very old, too."

"Oh, Mama..." Emma started to cry. "I'm worried about the elephants. Thabo says that they are disappearing from the earth. That the beautiful pendant you and Dad gave me is made of ivory. How can I wear it? He showed me a picture of a baby elephant whose mother was killed for her tusks. His father's sanctuary rescued it. Even then she may not live. If it's not safe for a little elephant in her own home in the jungle, where *is* it safe?"

"Who is this Thabo?"

"A new friend. He's from Africa and he's staying here at Astor Court. His father is going to speak at the United Nations."

Her mother sat down next to Emma on the piano bench and put her arms around her.

"Oh, my Emma! What a smart and loving person you are! Yes, we must try to protect the earth and all its wonderful creatures. The question is, how? In the meantime, here is how the left hand should sound."

As her mother played the Bach prelude—and so superbly—Emma couldn't help but wonder if music like this would heal the aching heart of a little elephant.

6

* * *

Later that morning, Emma met Thabo in the Astor Court garden. She told him she'd had the most vivid dream. She dreamt that Butterfly had come to New York City and was looking for Thabo and for a safe place to grow up.

"There must be a place in the USA where an elephant would be safe and happy. Should we check out the zoo?" asked Emma. "I haven't been there since I was little—I don't know what it's like now."

Thabo was surprised and pleased that Emma cared so much about Butterfly's well-being. He had never given much thought to how elephants live in the United States. Maybe this information would be helpful to his father when he spoke at the United Nations. He would be glad to go to the zoo. Somewhere he had seen a flyer advertising that there were three elephants living there—Cheery and Trouble and Turnip. They took the train uptown—in the same way they had in Emma's dream, minus the baby elephant in tow—and followed a group of tourists past the subway station heading toward the zoo.

At the zoo they stood on tiptoe, leaning this way and that, trying to catch a glimpse. It looked like there was only one elephant out that day, and she was having some foot treatment. The caregivers, a man in gray and a teenager in white with a blond braid down her back, were kneeling at the elephant's right front foot.

Emma couldn't believe her eyes and excitedly called out, "Angelina!"

The teenager, Angelina, waved hello and said that she would be right there. Emma whispered to Thabo that Angelina was a friend. She loved animals and had taught Emma a lot about them. Emma said that, oddly enough, Angelina always turned up when Emma was trying to solve a problem with an animal.

When Angelina finished helping the elephant's caretaker, she made her way over to the fence where Emma and Thabo were waiting. Emma introduced Thabo and told Angelina about their quest to find a safe place for Butterfly to grow up. Thabo showed her Butterfly's photo on his cell phone.

"What an adorable baby elephant," exclaimed Angelina. "She looks like the newborn I saw on TV at a Midwest zoo. It's true that there aren't any poachers or anything, but zoo's aren't the same as nature. They try hard here to make the animals' lives as interesting and natural as they can. But there's something in elephants that always wants to roam free."

She got permission from Sam, the keeper, for them to meet Cheery, the elephant. They would have to stay behind a double fence, but it was closer than what was allowed for the public. Cheery had been down in the dumps, Angelina told them, and she hoped their visit might lift her spirits.

As Angelina escorted them, they saw that part of the elephants' living quarters was outdoors, which gave the elephants a sense of nature. And part of it was indoors in concrete enclosures with large cages—that part wasn't too natural.

Sam nodded to the visitors and kept working on Cheery. He was scraping the underside of her foot. "Why is he doing that?" asked Thabo, who'd never seen Bitri do anything like that with the elephants back home.

Angelina explained that feet are a problem with captured elephants. In the wild they are known to walk ten to thirty miles a day looking for food and water. And so the soles of their feet are kept in shape. In captivity, scraping and sanding the bottoms had to be done for them, and their nails had to be trimmed. Otherwise, the elephants' feet would become sore and infected. They would experience joint problems and arthritis and could even become crippled.

Angelina looked affectionately toward the large elephant.

"Cheery, I brought some friends," she said, gesturing to Sam to bring Cheery close to the double fence. "This is Thabo, all the way from Africa. He helps take care of orphaned baby elephants. You remember being a baby once, don't you?"

Cheery walked slowly over and blinked a couple of times.

"And this is my dear friend, Emma," Angelina continued. Emma smiled and gently waved her hand in greeting. Emma hadn't been so close to an elephant before. There she was, almost nose-to-trunk with this majestic creature. She felt the power of the elephant's size. Unwittingly, she reached out to touch Thabo's sleeve as if to bring herself back to earth. For when she looked into Cheery's eyes, it was as if Emma had become an elephant, too. She saw in her mind's eye Cheery and herself free, living in a herd with elephant relatives. There was the blue sky overhead and the wild plains stretching before them. In her imagination, Cheery's whole body was transformed from sagging and listless into a robust expression of joy, and Emma was running beside her. Clouds of dust kicked up behind them from the dry ground in the heat of the afternoon sun.

Cheery blinked some more and raised her trunk.

"Cheery's really a sweetheart," said Angelina. "Let me tell you her story. A couple of research scientists put a full-length mirror in Cheery's living quarters and drew a smiley face on her skin above her eyebrow in white ink. She touched her smiley face almost fifty times with her trunk. Because she recognized herself in the mirror, the scientists knew she was really smart. It looked like she was fixing her makeup." Emma and Thabo smiled.

"And Cheery became famous. Her video went viral. Scientists and reporters were writing articles about her. She was a celebrity. But it was so sad—in the middle of all of this, Cheery's friend Dreary passed away. The other two elephants here, Turnip and Trouble, kinda stick to themselves. Cheery's heart is aching now, and she's lonely."

"Well, we think you are smart and beautiful, Cheery. We don't want you feeling down in the dumps," said Thabo. He gently reached up to pet Cheery, but he could only touch the fence. The elephant didn't understand the words he was saying, but she understood something in another way, and Cheery slowly pressed herself up against the fence and lifted her trunk to Thabo's hand.

"I wish you could stay with us," said Angelina.

Thabo imagined himself an elephant living with Cheery in the zoo. He knew that even though he would be making children and their families happy, he would want his freedom. That's just the way that elephants were.

Emma had almost forgotten her dream from the night before, but now she turned pale as she remembered the elephants in the circus and felt Cheery's sadness behind the double fence in front of her. "Let's head back," she told Thabo, who looked at her, concerned, and took her hand.

7

* * *

Emma and Thabo were enjoying their hummus, let-
tuce, and tomato sandwiches in the Astor Court garden. Thabo was saying how much he liked New York City.
Maybe Emma could visit him in Africa? Their sanctuary
was quite different from the city, but he thought she'd
enjoy meeting all the animals. It was hard for Emma to
imagine being that far from home. Thabo knew so much
more of the world than she did.

"What about a sanctuary in the United States for
Butterfly? There are no poachers here," said Emma.

Thabo hadn't even realized that there were sanctuaries in the United States. "I guess we could Google 'elephant sanctuaries' and see if there are any." He took out
his new cell phone. It turned out that there were quite a
few. He showed Emma a couple of them. And then they
looked at the resident elephants.

"Here's an African elephant like Butterfly," Thabo
said, showing her the screen. "There are only about four

hundred thousand left in the wild. And Cheery, the one we saw at the zoo today, is Asian. I think there are only about forty thousand Asian elephants in the wild. Those sound like big numbers, but it's very small compared to what it used to be."

They read the description of a resident named Daisy: "A forty-four-year-old elephant, had been in a circus in Palm Beach, a zoo in Texas, then in a movie, then another zoo, and was rescued..."

And then Dinky, an Asian elephant: "Sold to the exotic animal trade as a youngster, in a zoo for thirty years, was not cooperative, was sweet and sociable in the sanctuary..."

And Delilah, another Asian elephant: "Born in Thailand, twenty-four years in the circus, twenty-two years in the zoo, came to the sanctuary crippled..."

"It looks like the sanctuaries here are for exhausted elephants," said Thabo. "These are wonderful havens, but they aren't for young ones. We would like Butterfly to have everything a young elephant needs—a mother, elephants her age to play with, and the chance to grow up and have a family of her own. She has that at my father's sanctuary in Africa, but poachers will be waiting in the bushes when she is released back into the wild."

And then Thabo's cell phone rang. It was Bitri from Africa on Skype, calling from the nursery for baby elephants. Butterfly wasn't drinking her formula. Bitri said that Thabo should come home to his father's sanctuary right away. Butterfly could only last another two days if she didn't start to eat again. Thabo's leaving was just too much for her.

"Please put the phone where she can hear me," said Thabo.

"Okay," said Bitri.

There was Butterfly lying on her side in her nursery stall. She was breathing heavily and looked as if she had given up the wish to live. Even the tufts of hair on her head were drooping.

"Butterfly, I'm coming back home. Hang on, Butterfly. Hang on tight. I love you. It'll be all right."

"She opened her eyes, Thabo," said Bitri. "There's not a lot of time."

"I'll be there."

Thabo ended the call and turned to Emma. "You see, Emma, I have to go back! It's a good thing we were leaving tonight anyway. But come with me to the UN to hear my father's talk. Maybe it will help you understand. You would have to return to Astor Court on your own, if that's Okay."

"Let me ask my parents," said Emma. "I'll be right back."

***

Because Thabo was the son of the speaker, he and Emma were allowed in the back of the hall while Thabo's father gave his talk.

"Your father doesn't look anything like you."

"He was born in England. He came from London to Kenya as a journalist and stayed. Shhh...listen."

To sum up—there is an elephant in the room, ladies and gentlemen, wherever you live, and whatever language you speak. And that elephant is crying out to each one of us, "Protect me. Time is running out." Are we listening, ladies and gentlemen? Tusks don't just fall out of elephants— these animals are being massacred at an alarming rate for their ivory.

There is a light that shines within every living being. If we allow the light of the elephant to be extinguished, our planet will be a darker place. Once again, I urge you to form stricter laws against elephant poaching, and enforce them. And I urge you to sow the seeds of compassion in your children.

Let us work together for a sustainable future. We need funding for more guards to protect the national parks. We need to create new ways for the impoverished in your nations to earn their living. Let us see to it that your people and the elephants have a future.

And please come to our sanctuary and wildlife preserve as our guests.

Thank you, ladies and gentlemen.

There was a loud buzzing in many different languages after the talk. Everyone in the room seemed energized. Emma wondered how they understood one another, speaking in such different ways.

"Oh, Thabo!" said Emma. "Thank you for bringing me here. I must do something. I know you and your father are doing all you can. Children can help too. Maybe I can start by talking to one person a day about elephants. I can tell them about poachers and the ivory trade, and about elephants in captivity."

Thabo took her hands in his and nodded. "Unless we change our hearts and ways, there is no safe place for elephants. What happens to elephants affects all of us."

Thabo promised to stay in touch via e-mail and Skype. Before leaving, he wanted to give her something. Thabo handed Emma a gift wrapped in gold paper.

"It's a framed photo of Butterfly."

Emma pressed it to her heart. "A live elephant is better than an ivory necklace any day."

"Bye for now, Emma," said Thabo. "I bet your name means *brave* in American."

Emma's cheeks got rosy red. "Bye for now, Thabo." She threw her arms around him and held him tight for a moment. Then, both embarrassed, they stood gazing at one another, not knowing what to say or how to say it—two young people from opposite ends of the world brought together by fate and their love for animals. And then Thabo gave her a thumbs-up and walked to where his father was waiting for him at the door.

8

* * *

Emma's dad was just finishing his coffee when Emma came into the kitchen the next morning. Vice presidents of corporations always seemed to be rushing someplace. He grabbed his overcoat from the chair.

"Hi, Punkin!" He bent down to kiss her good-bye.

"It's *pumpkin!* And don't call me that, anyway."

"Uh-oh, my girl doesn't sound so good this morning. Mom tells me that you're worried about elephants. Is that it? She says you want a piano with plastic keys."

"I'm worried about Butterfly."

"Who is Butterfly?"

"The little orphaned elephant at the sanctuary in Africa. My friend, Thabo, and his father flew home last night to try to save her."

"I'm sorry, Emma," said her dad.

"How can we get people to see what they probably don't want to?"

Her dad stopped short and sat down again. "Well, in the advertising business, we say that you have to get to people where they live. You've got to try to make them *feel* something a little different. If you can do that, it might help them change their behavior. What do you want them to see and feel?"

"I want them to see that elephants are very intelligent and sensitive. They live in families and seem to know more about helping each other than we do. And we are killing them off for stupid trinkets, jewelry, and statues!"

Dad was quiet for a moment. "You know, maybe you should try writing something. Get something down. If we like it, I'll help you get it out there." He got up again to go.

"But I don't know how to start!"

"Well, you know what your mother says. 'The heart speaks, the head edits.'"

"What does that mean?"

"It means that you get quiet, and let what you care about fill you. The words will come naturally." He kissed the top of her head, then ruffled her hair. "Gotta go now. Bye, my punk—Sorry! My wonderful Emma."

Emma picked up the scratch pad that was used for the family's grocery list.

She stared at it for a long moment. What would make people feel different about elephants? Nothing was coming to her. And then she remembered that first day in the garden with Thabo. How he had shown her a picture of Butterfly and how moved she had been. She ran to get her photo of Butterfly and brought it back to the kitchen table. She gazed at the small elephant's face, and suddenly Butterfly began to speak to her heart...

I dream that all the killing will stop and that baby elephants will be able to grow up without fear...

9

* * *

As soon as their land rover approached the sanctuary compound, Thabo jumped out and ran toward the nursery. The sun was just coming up. His father called to him.

"Thabo, please! You've been up most of the night. You didn't eat anything on the plane. Come in the house for a few minutes and at least get a piece of toast."

But Thabo was only thinking about one thing.

The barn was cool and dark. There, in Butterfly's stall, a terrible sight greeted him. Bitri sat on the on the straw, his back propped up against the side of the stall. He held Butterfly in his arms.

The little elephant was wrapped in the gray blanket used to suggest the mother's body. Only her head was visible. But Thabo could tell right away that Butterfly was not doing well. Despite Bitri's efforts, she was shivering uncontrollably. The skin on her face and ears was dry and loose. Her eyes were half closed. She looked as though she had given up hope.

"She hasn't taken the bottle for several days," said Bitri sadly. "She's lost a lot of weight. She is badly dehydrated."

"Butterfly, I'm back," cried Thabo. "Please, don't leave us!"

"Thabo snuggled in under the blanket, and began to sing softly to her, the way he had seen Bitri do. "Please, please get better, Butterfly. I love you. And there are so many people who care about you and want you to be well and happy. And there's this girl in New York. Her name is Emma, and when I told her about you, she started dreaming about you. And we went all over the place looking for a safe home for you."

It was quite a sight: two human animals sending warmth and love to a little animal of another species.

At first, there was no response. The baby just sighed deeply. Despite himself, Thabo began to cry. He was afraid that crying wasn't very manly, but he couldn't help himself. And then something unexpected happened. Butterfly, too, began to cry. Tears rolled down her cheeks, staining her face. She lifted her head to look at Thabo.

"There are all kinds of tears," said Bitri. "Those are tears of joy."

Thabo hugged Butterfly with all his might and she began to respond.

She began to move a little. She wrapped her trunk around Thabo, just like in the dream that Emma had described.

"I think we may be in luck," said Bitri. "I'm going to get some formula."

10

* * *

Emma had waited days for this moment. Her dad had gotten Skype up and ready to go on the computer, and then had diplomatically left the room.

And suddenly, all the way from Africa, there he was. Thabo's eyes were shining.

"She's going to make it!" he said.

11

*** * ***

In Africa, the morning sun was rising. The heavy rains prepared the way. Every leaf and blade of grass glistened with dew. Another baby elephant was born. And a rainbow appeared in the sky. After twenty-two months of growing inside his mother, it was time to stand in a new world.

The elephants danced in slow motion to a song from the beginning of time.

The song of life.

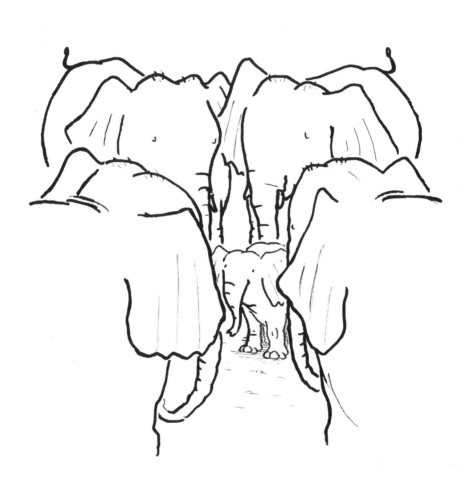

Friends of Butterfly

Ainsley Paget Brown, Margaret Zox Brown,
Gretchen Burnett, Paula Greller, Mary Hamill,
Gerhard Holt, Ingrid Hong, Susan Irving, Bill Kosmas,
Zohra Lampert, Deborah Landey, Linda Langton,
Gabriela Marx, Jack Pettey, Lynne Rosenthal,
Brad Rothschild and family, Maya Salvana,
Rita Fredricks Salzman, Penelope Bodry Sanders,
Heidi Shalloway, Doris Solomon, Chris Stover,
Renee Sytwu, Tatiana Timanovskaia, Allan Wagner,
Mark Wilk.

Special Thanks
to

The Editors of Butterfly

About the Authors
and Artist

Marian Hailey-Moss is vegan and an animal activist. The eight children's books she has authored are about people's relationship with animals. She lives in New York City.

Lois Meredith's passion for the well-being of elephants was the inspiration for Butterfly. She is an essayist, playwright, and screenwriter. She lives and writes in New York City

Marc Chalvin, a Parisian who fills his drawings and his animations with life, whimsy, and wisdom.

Made in the USA
Charleston, SC
04 January 2015